A Big Night in Booville

Written by
Slade Stone

Illustrated by
John Jordan
Jerry Brent Dillingham

All art and text ©Dalmatian Press.
ISBN: 1-57759-834-2
First published in the U.S. in 2002 by Dalmatian Press, LLC, U.S.A.

Dalmatian Press

02 03 04 NGS 5 4 3 2 1

C0-BEJ-695

"It's a big night in Booville!" cheered Wilson as he hopped out of bed. And it was! It was Halloween. But more importantly—oh, much more importantly—it was Wilson's birthday!

Wilson straightened his wraps. Then, in the wee hours of the morning, he hurried over to Frank Junior's house.

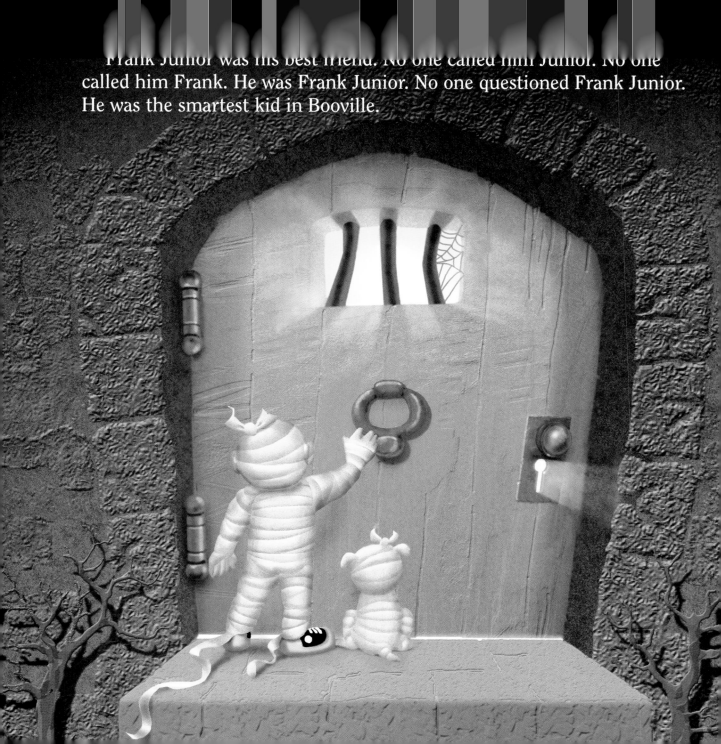

Frank Junior was his best friend. No one called him Junior. No one called him Frank. He was Frank Junior. No one questioned Frank Junior. He was the smartest kid in Booville.

"Hey, tonight's a big night!" exclaimed Wilson when Frank Junior opened the door.

"Indeed!" said Frank Junior. "It's a night of shenanigans and sweet confections and..."

"No, I mean...," started Wilson.

"He means 'tricks and treats!' " Frank Junior's sister came waltzing up to the door. "I don't know *why* you use such big words, Frankie."

"It's Frank Junior, if you please," her brother stated.

"OK, Frank Junior—Mr. Smartie!" Francine smirked. "Well, hello, Wilson. You look frightfully handsome for Booville's big night!"

Wilson stood up straight. "Why, thank you. I didn't know you knew this was a big night."

"Big night? It's the *best* night!" exclaimed Francine. "It's the most glamorous, spookiest, screamiest night of the year!"

"Well, I don't know about *that,*" said Wilson, blushing all the way though his wrappings.

"After all," said Francine, smoothing her hair,
"it's Halloween. And I'll have the best costume. Of course."

"Oh, of course. Halloween," Wilson said droopily.
"*That's* why it's a big night..."

Wilson stayed and played "Creepy Crawly Cards" and "Roll the Knuckles" with Frank Junior all day. And not once—not once!—did Frank Junior say Happy Birthday to Wilson. It was *definitely* time to go.

"Say—what are *you* going to be—uh—tonight, Frank Junior?" said Wilson.

"I've decided to don the look of a mad scientist. That way I can wear the new wig I created out of polymorpho fibers. It glows in the dark. What are you going as?"

"I dunno," sighed Wilson. "Maybe a ghost. Maybe a fish. I better go home and think about it. I'll see ya."

"Good-bye! I'll see you tonight for Halloweening!" called Frank Junior.

"I'll see you, too, Wilson! I'll be with Frankie!" sang out Francine.

"It's Frank *Junior*," her brother grumbled.

Wilson kicked a bone down the sidewalk.
"My very best friend. Ha! My best friend forgot this is my birthday. How could *anyone* forget that my birthday is Halloween? Every year, my friends throw me a party—and here it is—the very day—the big day—and no party plans!"

"Hey, Wilson!"
Wilson looked up. Here came Denton at full speed on his super speedy racing bike! To Wilson's horror, Denton was coming straight at him! He closed his eyes!
SCREEEEECH!

Wilson peeped out. There was Denton, smiling at him.
"Hey, bandage brain!" said Denton. "Ya know it's a big
night in Booville."
Wilson perked up. "Yes, it is!"

"Yeah, man. It's the night my dad lets me stay up 'til two o'clock and feed the bats!"

"Oh, yeah," sighed Wilson. "That sure is a big night."
He watched Denton zip off down the sidewalk.

"Bigger than *my* night will be...,"
he said to himself.

Wilson sat down on the grass and wiped his eyes. Then he did what he *always* did when he needed to think. He wrote himself some notes.

He felt lonely and forgotten. Wasn't there anyone who remembered that *this* was his birthday?

Rattle, clink, rattle, clink.

Just then, Kate skipped over and plopped down next to Wilson.

"Why, Wilson," she said sweetly, "what are you doing here? It's going to be a big night in Booville, you know."

"Yes, I know," said Wilson quietly. "It's Halloween. A night of tricks and treats and candy and howls and growls and catching bats..."

Kate giggled. "Oh, silly. It's a *much* bigger night than
that. I know a great secret! Come on and I'll show you!
You won't want to miss out on this!"

Wilson got up and followed Kate. "I really just want to go home," he told her.
"Well, OK. I'll walk you home—and then I'll show you the secret."
Wilson walked slowly behind Kate.
Who cares about her silly ol' secret? he
thought. *Even* she *forgot my birthday.*
And she's the nicest kid in Booville.

As Wilson came up to his own
front door, it slowly creaked open—

—and out popped a mad scientist, a movie star, and a wolfman!

"Surprise! Happy Birthday!"

"That's the secret," giggled Kate. "We're throwing the party at *your* house this year!"

"Yeah! What took ya so long?" said Denton. "Open your presents and cut the cake! Then we can all go out trick-or-treating

—and scare the neighborhood!"

It was a wonderful party with streamers and cake and punch and presents to unwrap. Wow! It was a *great* big night in Booville!